AFTER MIDNIGHT

THE NEVER AFTERS

Burnt Sugar

The New Wife

After Midnight

Braid

By The Moon's Good Grace

Winterbloom

AFTER MIDNIGHT

A NEVER AFTERS TALE

KIRSTYN MᶜDERMOTT

Brain Jar Press
PO Box 6687
Upper Mt Gravatt, QLD, 4122
Australia
www.BrainJarPress.com

After Midnight Copyright © 2022 by Kirstyn McDermott

The moral right of Kirstyn McDermott to be identified as the author of this work has been asserted.

Cover design by Peter Ball
Cover Image: *Broken Tiara*, Yavdat/Shutterstock

ISBN: 978-1-922479-36-5 (Ebook) | 978-1-922479-35-8 (Chapbook)

AFTER MIDNIGHT

And so it comes to this: sequestered in one of the guest wings of the palace, where my stepsisters have stayed before me, while SHE is safely ensconced in my own chambers. The *Queen's* Chambers — but although HER son may indeed be King one day, SHE shall never be Queen. ~~Not while I breathe~~.

Perhaps those are not words I should commit to paper, lest the Fates be tempted too sorely.

I have been told nothing about HER other than what SHE has in HER belly. The future of the kingdom, my husband insists. It would be no small irony indeed if what came out in the end was nothing more than another squalling girl-child, as useless as he deems the three daughters I have given him.

No, not useless, not entirely: he has already married off H—, our eldest, to cement an alliance in the west; negotiations for the hand of L— remain unresolved but promising. As for dear little S—, I fear she will end her days a spinster. Even now, although nine years of age, she can barely speak a sensible sentence and has proven a dullard when it comes to learning her letters. She can count and, in fact, counting is almost all that she does with her days — counts the flowers in the garden, the tiles on the floor in the hall, the boiled eggs that are brought to the table for breakfast. If she were prettier, her proclivities might not prove an obstacle but, with her flat features and perpetual scowl, she has only her father's name to recommend her — and who will care overly about the third princess in line once there is a prince waiting to ascend the throne?

No, she will likely remain with me until the end of her days. Or mine.

"You are Queen," my husband assured me. "You will always be Queen." Not, *my* Queen, I note. He has not called me that for many a year.

Oh, there have been others — pretty girls with hope and fancy in their eyes; silly girls easily appeased by a fistful of gold once he tires of them. There may even have been other illegitimacies, although I have been spared the knowledge of them. I have had my dalliances as well, of course. There is no shortage of fine young men with honour enough to guarantee silence.

We have been discreet, my husband and I. Although the first bloom of love may have faded as fast as a midnight frost, we have no wish to humiliate each other nor to bring suspicion upon our alliance. He was once the Prince who lifted me from the hearth, brushed the ashes from my skirts and restored me to my true station — he has always recognised my worth.

Besides, there are too few ways to rid oneself of an unwanted Queen, especially one who has cultivated the adoration of her subjects, who has inspired story after fanciful story of pumpkins turned to coaches and mice to prancing horses.

Even one whose womb has borne no fruit for almost a decade.

It is the perfect subterfuge, my husband says. This girl, according to both the wise woman whose head will roll if she is wrong and the King's physician whose head will remain neatly atop his shoulders no matter the outcome, this girl carries a *son*. An heir. The bloodline must flow forward, and my husband is unready to relinquish power to his cousin, already furnished with three strapping boys. *His* children should inherit the crown, he has said many a time. It should be *his* children, *his* grandchildren, with no shadow cast over succession.

For my part, I understand too well the need to employ all

means an end may justify. If I had been in my stepmother's shoes all those years ago, I too may have butchered the feet of my daughters in order to place them upon the very throne where I have found a perch. At the side of the King, I am safe. I am powerful. I am assured of neither sweeping a hearth nor counting a single lentil ever again. Would that not be worth a pesky toe or two?

Enough of such thoughts. Dinner is late and my stomach pinches. A guest in this wing has never been treated so ill before, I warrant. But I shall wait until the sun has completely set before ringing the bell a second time. I have learned nothing if not patience over the course of my life. Patience, and timing.

G— herself brought me my meal last night, having been the only one of my Ladies to have been retained. In service to the Royal Family for most of her life, I suppose she has been deemed the most trustworthy.

The girl has been furnished with an entirely new retinue, a trio of young women from across the sea who speak barely a word of our tongue but whose lands are famed for their advances in midwifery. It is a plausible enough story for Court, or so we hope — a long awaited conception followed by complications and thus a prolonged but necessary confinement. The midwives, naturally, will be dismissed the moment the child is born — the moment *before* he is placed into my waiting arms. Paid well for their services and their secrecy — if indeed they even suspect the secret they keep — and waved off home.

I enquired of G— as to HER health. Does SHE sicken in the morning as I did with all three of my girls? Do HER ankles grow fat? Has SHE the butterfly rash that ruddied my face with each of my pregnancies?

"SHE does well enough, Majesty," was all G— would say. Was it my imagination, or did that *Majesty* have an edge to it? Although I pressed her, as she brushed out my hair and readied me for bed, she continued to deflect my questions about all that goes on in the Queen's Chambers, of all that SHE does with HER days.

SHE does well enough, Majesty.

"It's only four more moons," G— told me with a smile I could not decipher.

Four moons! I took but three nights to hook my Prince's heart. What could SHE do with so much time? ~~What could~~

No. I must stop this. I am the Queen. Mother of the Princesses. Soon to be Mother of the Prince and Heir Apparent, whom I will raise as my own flesh and blood ~~if it kills me~~. My own flesh and blood — I can afford nothing less. When it comes to being a stepmother, however secret the role, I have had ample tuition in what *not* to do. ~~And even if she~~

No, I will not write it down. I will not even think it.

I am Queen. *I will always be Queen.* Woe betide any STRUMPET who seeks to dislodge me from my throne.

I have checked — they have not locked the door to this wing, although there is a guard posted outside the door. He stood to attention when I poked out my head and stuttered a nervous, "M'lady?" before I ducked back inside. He is young, that guard, and he has a pretty face. Clearly a fresh recruit. I do not know whether to be affronted by the assumption that I require a mere child to keep me in place, or relieved. But of course, he is here to ensure that no curious soul enters these quarters, rather than preventing myself from leaving them. I wonder who they have told him it is that he guards. If I desired it, I could wait until the lad grows drowsy and dim. It would be nothing to slip past him then.

But some cards are best kept in hand.

At least these rooms are warm. I have stoked the fire well, using the logs that G— piled beside the hearth earlier this evening. It is not work for a *Queen* but one does not entirely forget the skills of one's youth, no matter how repellent their memory.

Still, I wish I were in my rightful chambers. The windows to the south overlook the Queen's Garden and allow for a view of the hazel tree that I ordered moved there from my father's house. ~~She~~ It does not seem to have thrived as ~~she~~ it did where it was first planted, but I could not bear to leave ~~her~~ it behind when I came to live in the palace. The pigeons that once nested in its branches flew away years ago. Perhaps the tree misses them, and pines. I wish I could see it now. I wish I could steal out into the moonlight and press my brow against its trunk.

Tomorrow, I will demand that the remainder of my library be brought to these rooms. I am certain that SHE will not be in need of it. I doubt very much that SHE has even been taught her letters.

They have brought less than a quarter of my books.

G— said the removal of any greater number from the Queen's chambers might cause suspicion. I did not care for the manner in which she spoke, not meeting my eye, as she arranged them on their little shelf.

I am certain that she is keeping something from me.

The strangest thing — last night, in the middle of the night, I was awakened by a sharp pain in my foot. I sat myself up and saw, by the guttering light of the fire, a movement beneath the bedclothes. Then came another pain, like the bite of a small, sharp-toothed creature and I admit to crying out in surprise. I whipped off the coverings and there, perched with its little paws together in an attitude of prayer, was a rat. He was a large fellow, with a streak of silver down his spine.

I am not afraid of vermin, but nor did I wish to suffer another nip, and so I moved to kick my furry visitor away. The curious, bright-eyed expression with which it held my gaze, however, gave me pause. Head cocked to one side, the rodent wrinkled its nose at me then made a high-pitched chittering noise and scampered from the bed to vanish into the shadows beneath it.

Only then did I see what it had left behind.

The ring was the one my mother had given me before she died. It had been her mother's ring before her and I had worn it on a chain about my neck until my father remarried. My stepmother, catching sight of it one morning as I cleaned, deemed the thing too precious for a child to wear as a mere bauble and took it away — for safe-keeping, she said. I had not laid eyes on it since. I have no idea how the rodent came by the ring, nor why it decided to return it to me. It sits easily on my index finger now and I like how the small ruby in its setting sparkles when I hold it to the light.

Regardless, I made sure to remove it when G— came with my breakfast. The woman has a sharp eye and a mind made to keep inventory; she would spot the ring immediately and know it had not come from the Queen's Jewels. Then she would ask questions and might mention it to someone else, to my husband even. But it is my ring, and I would keep it a secret. The Queen should be allowed a secret or two, although heaven knows it has been years since my every possession, my every step and sigh, was solely my own.

I inquired after my stepmother and G— gave me a surprised glance. Why did I care to know about that woman, she wanted to know. As far as she was aware, my stepmother was still living with my father, growing ever poorer under his roof and withering title.

"But has she not paid a visit to the palace recently?" I asked.

"Not since the royal wedding," G— said.

I smiled to hear it. My stepmother knows how unwelcome she is and would not dare curry further disfavour.

I am glad to have my mother's ring once more, whatever the means by which it reached me. Later, I shall ask to be escorted to the Queen's Garden. I wish to visit the hazel tree. It is spring; perhaps the birds have returned.

The rat continues to bring me gifts, waking me in the witching hour with a nibble on my toes. Pieces of jewellery from my own collection — not ones that I had worn often, but still mine — among others I do not recognise. Gold rings and bracelets, studded with gems; necklaces and chokers, both ornate and plain. Even a brooch that appears to be carved from jet. I dare not wear any of it. There is, however, a small compartment in my dresser and I have hidden it all inside, beneath one of my embroidered shawls.

Despite my demands, I have not been permitted to leave these rooms, even briefly. When my husband first came to me with his plans, we discussed such matters and decided that I would be allowed a modest walk of the grounds at dawn or at dusk — alone and incognito — so that I might take in the fresh air — but this has not yet come to pass.

G— is adamant that there is too great a risk. I might be seen and recognised. She reminds me, as though I am a simpleton, of the ruse in which we all now take part, so necessary to protect the future heir, my future *son*. No one outside the innermost circle of the court must know that I am not the child's mother.

"The Crown must be secure," she says.

"Your husband has enemies," she says.

"Any whiff of illegitimacy would be a threat," she says.

I have heard these words so many times; they are beginning to wear thin to my ears.

I fear I will go insane in these rooms. This morning I burst into tears for no reason while G— dressed my hair. ~~I could not stop crying~~. She appeared frightened and tried to comfort me. I have crescents in my palms, so tightly did I clench my fists.

But one good thing has come of it — my husband visited with me this afternoon for almost an hour. We sat and he held my hand in his and told me again that he worried for me and that it pained his heart to see me so fretful. I would always be Queen, he assured me, I would always be the mother to his children — *all* of his children — and I had nothing to fear. Three more moons and this confinement would be over. Three more moons and I would have a new baby boy to love. A new baby *prince*.

Did I not realise how important my role would be? Mother to the Prince. His eyes were kind as he pleaded with me.

"Why can SHE not be here instead?" I found myself asking. I hated the whine in my voice. I shudder, even now, to remember it. But I continued nevertheless — why should I be the one banished from my own chambers, from my beloved garden and the rest of the palace, while SHE is free to roam at will? It was not fair.

My husband frowned and regarded me as though I were a child.

He assured me that SHE is not free, any more than I am. SHE is confined to the Queen's Chamber, as much as I am confined to these accommodations, with rumours of ill health spread daily. HER new ladies in waiting are the only ones to see HER, with the King's physician as intermediary, and he leads them to believe that the woman they wait upon is the Queen.

"No one must know, my darling. It is the most important secret you will ever keep."

I felt foolish, the blood rushing to my cheeks. I knew this, every word of it. How could I have forgotten? While he was here, I felt calm and reassured. I could look into his eyes and see only sincerity and warmth. The strength I have always seen in him. But now my rooms are empty and I find myself fretting once more. ~~If only~~

Part of me wishes I had not agreed to this subterfuge. I had not expected the confinement to be such a trial. I wish I had my daughters with me — even S— would be a comfort, if not a thrilling conversationalist. I hope they are all happy on their tour abroad and that their tutors and governess are taking good care of them. But I also hope that they miss me as I miss them, and that they think of me as they lie on their pillows each night, and keep me in their prayers.

Me, and their soon-to-be little brother.

If I am not to leave these rooms until the birth, I think I shall go mad with only my own company to keep. I told G— as much and she merely smiled.

"Your own company is fine company," she said. "Anybody would be glad of it."

. . .

I have read all the books.

I am sick to death of embroidery.

I find myself sleeping too much and too soundly, woken only by the nibble of a rat's tooth on my toes, or the gentle shake of a shoulder by G— when she brings me my meals.

"Do you attend upon HER so solicitously?" I asked of her this morning.

"I attend upon her as she needs, Majesty."

"And does my husband attend up on HER also? As she needs?"

G—paused at that, before saying that I must not fret myself to pieces. The King attends upon HER daily, I was told, as propriety demands. What would the palace think if he did not visit his ill Queen during her confinement? G— assures me that I need not to worry. All is proceeding to plan.

I am trying not to worry.

But it has never been *my* plan. I merely acquiesced to play my part.

The rats have not been to visit for days. It is strange to write it, but I find myself missing them.

Of all the unexpected things — a visit from my younger step-sister!

Balancing a heavily laden tea-tray, G— escorted her to my rooms this evening. Even hidden beneath a veil and a cloak of midnight blue, I recognised M— by her tread before a word was even spoke, by that limp which has remained her whole life, despite the golden toe she had cast for herself after her marriage.

Why was she here, I demanded to know the moment that G— withdrew. I kept my voice low, not wishing the guard beyond the door to overhear.

"I have often visited you," she replied. "*Sister.*"

The emphasis on that last was not lost on me but I held my tongue, examining as I always do the shape of her nose, the furrow that deepens between her eyebrows whenever she frowns, even the shape of her fingers as they lift a teacup to her mouth. As the years pass, she looks more and more like me. Like my father. Like her father. We have never spoken of it directly but we both know the truth. A half-measure of the same blood runs through our veins; her older sister's as well, no doubt, although the resemblance is not as perceptible. Little wonder, then, that my father remarried so quickly after my mother's death. To a woman with many hard-worn years under her belt, no less, and two mewling daughters dragged along in her wake.

Both my step-sisters are older than me, a fact I have contemplated often. Why did he marry my mother if he loved another — loved her enough to bring her into his home after so many years apart? Did he love my mother at all? Was the match with her a more advantageous one?

I could ask him if I truly wished to know. But what has passed cannot be undone and forgiveness is only for those who ~~desire~~ deserve it. I do not count my father among that number. He who cast me aside as though I were naught but a soiled rag, or a stone that became stuck in his shoe during an ill-fated journey. My step-mother I can almost understand, coming into a second-hand nest with one scrappy chick left to tend — but my father, oh! My father turned his back and left me to her. Left me in the cinders and the ash, and then called me *filth*. No, not even in my mother's memory will I talk to that man again. Let him rot.

But come, I digress.

M— knows of the plot, it seems, having been instrumental in its architecture. SHE who bears my husband's son was employed in her very household! Came into this palace under her auspices! M— saw how my husband looked at the girl, took careful note no doubt, and when SHE began to show, sat HER down and questioned HER. It was M—, I learned, who brought the WRETCH here a second time, brought HER to my husband's attention once again. I am livid at the thought.

"I did not think this would come to pass," M— told me, gesturing to the room around us. The girl was a good maidservant and my step-sister only wanted to help HER. M— liked HER and hoped SHE would one day be her Lady's Matron.

The expectation was merely that the King would correct his error with coin enough to allow the girl to keep and care for the child — not that it would be stolen from HER under royal fiat. But my husband's physician stepped in with whispered words and, before M— could protest, the girl was whisked away.

"Why come to me?" I asked her coldly. "What benefit does it bring you?"

M— put down her teacup with care, although her fingers trembled and the cup clattered rudely against the saucer.

"You do not have to allow the situation to continue," she said. "You have the power to put a stop to it all and demand the girl go free."

I was taken aback by the sudden tears that glossed her eyes. My step-sister who, as a young woman, had taken a carving knife to her own toes in hope of securing a future for herself, weeping over a servant! Irritated, I demanded that she dispense with these ill-veiled lies and tell me the truth. What did she really want?

Lowering her head, M— dabbed at her eyes with a lace-trimmed handkerchief. "I love her," she said. "I would do anything for her." I can still hear the catch and shudder in her voice as she spoke those words.

"As a daughter," I ventured when I found my speech again. "As you would love a daughter?" My step-sister had proved barren after all; it would be no great shock to find her motherly affection spoiling for an object.

But M— merely held my gaze and said, again, "I love her. Not as a daughter; not as a sister."

There has been talk seeping from her household for years. I had her married off to an old, cantankerous Lord who, folks whispered snidely, cared more for hunting and drinking and gambling than he did for women. I herded both my step-sisters into marriages that would see them well-kept, and which would be advantageous to the Crown, but I cared little for what happiness might result. In truth, I took a certain satisfaction in seeing them attached to men I would not deign so much as to spit upon. Although there has been no issue from the marriage (unlike my older step-sister with her brood of six), Lord F—

seems not to care. He has brothers to whom his estate may pass, should there be anything left of it upon his death. My husband sits a card sharp at the gambling tables; much of Lord F—'s losses flow to the royal coffers. The arrangement is satisfactory to all.

I had dismissed the rumours that surrounded M— until now. A childless woman in a loveless marriage — of course there would be speculation of dalliances. Although the talk of pretty young chambermaids spending the night in her rooms ...

This evening, I looked into her face and knew the stories to be true.

Was she so lonely, I wanted to know, that she would seek solace in the arms of a girl? Were there no pretty boys in her household, no handsome young groom or guard to summon to her bed?

She smiled then, a chill and callow grin that I did not care to see. "Not at present," she replied. "But I shall make sure to install a worthy selection for when next you come to call."

I blushed at that, my cheeks growing hotter yet with annoyance. I hate to blush, or weep, or show any signs of weakness, especially before my step-sisters. My victory over them, and over my step-mother, is tarnished by such displays.

I told M— that there was nothing I could do, that what has been set in motion cannot now be stilled, not when the hand of the Crown itself drives it on. Why should she care, in the end? The girl would be returned to her in a matter of moons, empty-bellied and ready for the play-pen once more.

M— winced at that and, for the fleetest of moments, I regretted my cruelty. But she brought this upon herself; she brought it upon us all.

"You are not so naive," M— said in a low voice. "I know you are not."

"Neither are you," I retorted. Did she think that, even if I ~~could help them~~ helped them, she and the girl might run away like a pair of wayward lovers? That they might set up house and hearth to raise the baby together? I have heard of such *Sapphic* arrangements in other, less civilised, lands but not here. What did she think could come of my interference but a public flogging? Or worse?

M— narrowed her eyes. "Don't presume the hearts of others to be as mercenary as your own, sister." She assured me that the girl does indeed return her feelings, but even if that were not the case, it would make no difference to her actions now. SHE does not wish to surrender HER baby; this situation had been forced upon HER as much as it had on me. Surely I must see that? Surely I must too feel impelled to assist a young woman in need?

I stared at her, willing ice and steel into my gaze. "It is not HER baby to keep. 'Twas my husband's seed that planted it; by rights, he shall reap the harvest."

My step-sister left soon afterward, first gathering herself into her cloak and veil. She did not look at me again and I did not turn to see her leave but waited, spine straight, until I heard the door close softly behind her. Her accusations are preposterous! Of course the girl will be dismissed once ~~her the~~ my baby is born. With a purse full of gold, no doubt, and a head full of plans to seduce some ~~other foolish~~ unwitting wretch. Such girls forge careers lying upon their backs; this one is different only in that she will make delivery of a Prince. I would not have thought M— so foolish as to be seduced by such a creature.

I certainly am not.

G— arrived just now to assist me with my bath, but I sent her away. I do not wish to speak to her, nor to any other person. The jug of water she left behind grows cold beside the basin. I will not bathe tonight. I am Queen and can do as I wish.

The rat returned tonight and brought with him several friends. They nipped at my toes until I awoke, then scampered from the bed and scuttled over to the door where they waited with noses twitching, seeming for all the world like strange miniature dogs begging to be let outside. My toes were bleeding and left marks behind on the floor. The door, unlocked as always, opened almost soundlessly on its well-oiled hinges. The same young guard was slumped on the ground, dozing.

Carefully, following the lead of the rats, I tiptoed past him.

The palace was quiet, and cold. The little rodents led me through the halls, their claws clicking on the bare stone as they hugged the walls. I kept to the carpets that lined the centre of the halls, wishing that I had thought to wear my slippers. It was not long before we were near ~~the Queen's~~ my chambers. Peering around a corner, I could see two guards standing either side of the door; neither looked the slightest bit drowsy. I stepped back, uncertain, my mouth suddenly dry. But ~~one of the rats~~ the rat with the white stripe tugged at the hem of my nightgown, urging me back the way I had come. Dutifully, I followed the bold little creature and soon found myself facing a small, lamplit alcove that I must have passed a thousand times without notice. A framed tapestry hung on the recessed wall; autumn fruits stitched by a patient hand.

Several of the rats chittered below, half scrambling up the wall. The striped rat bit my toe again and I hissed at it, using much strength of will not to raise my foot and stomp the insolent creature flat. The rodent stared at me with bright dark eyes, then looked towards the tapestry and then, I swear, the little fellow *nodded*. Carefully, I lifted the frame from the wall — and gasped. Behind was a hole, no bigger than my wedding ring and shining with a pale yellow light. I pressed a cheek against the stone wall and peered through.

It was ~~the Queen's bedchamber~~ my bedchamber that I looked upon, with HER lying in my bed, lit by an array of candles. I could see her hair splayed on the pillow, her delicate hand clutching the coverlet. And oh! SHE looks like me! My pen shakes even as I put these words down, I am so overcome with ~~fear~~ anger. SHE could be my younger sister — not the cuckoos who came into my home after the death of my mother, but a *full-blooded* sister — or even a *younger* self.

She has the same yellow hair that was my pride before the grey came creeping in. The same figure too, I would warrant — wide of hip with a cinched-in waist so perfectly sized for a ~~princely~~ *kingly* hand to wrap about. Are HER eyes the same brilliant emerald green that I see in my looking glass? Have I judged wrong in thinking the girl so dispensable? Until I looked upon HER, I did not question my husband's interest in anything other than HER issue. ~~But what if he~~

I must remember — I have no friends in this palace. My ladies in waiting are all dismissed and there is only G— who has more loyalty to my husband and to *his* children — no matter the womb from which they spill — than to myself.

SHE looks like me. SHE

I had to leave off just now, to arise and pace and pace until the churning in my stomach quelled. For there is more here to record.

From my secret vantage in the alcove, I could view half the bedchamber. I felt ill then thinking of who else may know about this spyhole, of who may have watched me over the years, and what they might have witnessed. I did not tarry any longer but replaced the tapestry and hurried back to these dull quarters where I am now confined. No dozen fat candles to guard my sleeping self! No coverlet made of fine damask! ~~No~~

Still, be still. There is more.

The young guard was awake and emerging from my room as I rounded the corner. We almost bumped into each other and, startled, I struck his cheek.

What right did he have to enter my private rooms, I demanded to know. What was he seeking? On whose behalf?

The young man looked aghast. He had only nodded off for a moment, he stammered, but had woken to find the door ajar, only entering to ascertain my own safety after his knocking went unheeded. He swallowed hard, more nervous than I have ever known a grown man to be. He was only concerned for me, he said, and was exceedingly grateful to find me now returned, and unharmed.

I pressed a finger to his mouth. "You were asleep longer than a moment, dear boy; I have been gone half the night. What would your captain say if he knew how derelict you have been in your duty? Why, any brigand might have slipped by you and cut my throat!" The boy was ashen. He began to reply but I hushed him with a shake of my head. I would say nothing, I assured him, and neither would he. So long as the rats do not find sudden use of their tongues, who will know?

"We have a secret now," I whispered. "Do you know who it is that you protect, and why?"

"You—you are cousin to the Queen," he said.

"And so my secrets are hers as well." I leaned close and brushed my lips against his cheek. "It is quite a thing to keep a secret for a Queen, and to have her keep one for you."

There was relief in his face when I drew away, and also a spark of longing. Smiling at him, I held a finger to my lips and slipped back inside my quarters. Only then did I allow myself to crumble.

I have been spied upon.

The thought of unknown eyes peering into my bedchamber! I shall ensure my husband knows of the spyhole. I shall have him seal it before I return to

Unless he already knows. Knows and avails himself. Knows and

These quarters are dimly lit by moonlight and the remains of the fire. I have just spent the remainder of the night examining each and every inch of wall, removing every framed tapestry and painting — even rolling up the carpets. My hands spread themselves over every flat surface, including the backs of wardrobes, until, as dawn broke beyond my window, I felt satisfied that no similar spyholes looked upon my current habitations.

In here at least, I am on my own.

I am exhausted. My hands ache. From searching, and from writing all of this down lest I later doubt, and convince myself that it is a dream. I must sleep. I must not crumble any further.

It seemed I had barely closed my eyes when G— came bustling in with my breakfast tray, her round face aghast at the shambles that I have created.

"Are you ill, Majesty?" she asked. "Is this delirium?"

I managed to choke down the laughter that surged upwards. I was bored, I told her instead. There is nothing to do all day in these quarters and I wished to take a walk in the gardens. She was to tell my husband that I require fresh air, that my humours are disordered. That I might go mad if I am not able to see the sky.

G— looked very grave when she left. I believe that my wish may at last be granted.

I was brought a large sun-hat and a raggedy coat, as well as an old wooden cane. As we left my quarters, G— instructed me to stoop. "*Try* to stoop," rather, as though I might be unable accomplish such an outrageous feat of deception. No one must guess who I am, she insisted, offering her arm for me to which I was expected to cling. Assuming the manner of a creaky old crone, I shuffled by her side through the servant passages. Although we did not go through the kitchens, we passed near enough to hear the bustle of people within and catch the aroma of the ovens. My mouth watered.

It occurred to me then that I have never once set foot inside the palace kitchens, nor any kitchen at all since leaving my father's house. A part of me ached to see it. To plunge my fingers knuckle-deep in dough, to smell the rising bread. A foolish want, but still.

The Queen's Garden was quiet, as it usually is, and empty, with not even a solitary gardener in evidence. Vacated for my benefit, no doubt — or, more truly, for the benefit of the King and his precious secret. G— remained at the front gate. She had brought a little lacework with her and set herself upon a wooden bench. The woman's eyes must indeed be sharp for her age; her lacework is very fine and has not diminished in quality over the years. She made each of my daughters a handkerchief for their baptisms with their initials embroidered in cobalt blue — my husband's House colour. I realised that she must now be crafting a piece for ~~HER baby~~ my baby — *my baby* — I must say it again and again until it is true.

I left G— to her work and made my way to the middle of the garden where the hazel tree sulks, all stunted and sparse. There has been only a smattering of yellow flowers each spring and barely any nuts. Those that do grow each autumn have been small and stodgy, and bitter on the tongue.

I pressed my hand against the trunk and closed my eyes. I do not know what I expected; the tree has not spoken to me for years. Regardless, I felt better in her presence. Calmer. Stronger.

Less alone.

From behind me, there came a rustling sound and I turned in time to see a long, pink tail disappear around the side of the tree. I crawled after it and saw that a hole had been dug close to the trunk, between the roots. As I watched, a furry brown head peered out at me and squeaked once before vanishing again.

"I might have known you were behind them," I told the tree. "Run out of birds to do your bidding?" The tree was silent. Gathering my skirts, I sat down and leaned my back against the bark, in what I expect was a most *un*queenly fashion, and I thought about my daughters, away on their tour of the northern lands. I could not convince my husband to allow them to stay, although I would have dearly liked their company from time to time. But not even H—, who will soon be running her own household, can know the truth of our subterfuge.

Girls cannot help but gossip, my husband believes. For all their good intentions, they would tell someone, and that someone would tell someone and that is how forest fires begin. We cannot allow a single spark to fly free. I cannot deny that he is right. Women do gossip. Information is our currency, and our power. With what else do we have to barter in this world?

I must have dozed off at some point for G— had cause to wake me with an apologetic shake of my shoulder. The day was late and she had let time get away from her — she should have come for me well before now. Indeed, the shadows were long and my back spasmed as she helped me to my feet. There was a twig caught in my hair and G— pulled it gently free. She was about to toss the thing to the ground but I stopped her and she placed it upon my outstretched palm instead. I wanted to take a piece of the tree back with me to my rooms. It sits on the windowsill as I write this, thin and dry with a trio of small leaves at its tip.

We were almost out of the garden when I noticed HER. G—placed a cautioning hand on my wrist. She did not take hold — she would not have dared; not even her favour in my husband's household would have pardoned an attempt to physically restrain the Queen — but her voice was firm: "Please keep walking, Majesty. No good can come of this."

I paid no heed. I wanted once more to look upon SHE who has colonised my rightful chambers. I wanted to see HER face in the sunlight.

Moreover, I wanted HER to see mine.

For all my choleric fervour, I did not get within one hundred feet of HER before I froze. SHE was dressed in one of my favourite summer gowns, the one with the butter yellow trim and daffodils woven into the bodice. It had been altered to accommodate HER growing belly. The bonnet that SHE was wearing was unfamiliar, oversized as is the current fashion, but no doubt chosen to conceal HER visage from the casual observer — as was the netting that hung from its rim. SHE was flanked by HER trio of midwives and it was this that gave me pause. I could not let them see me — the risk was too great. G— was right. My husband was right. We have built too flimsy a screen behind which to hide; it would take but a breath to blow it asunder.

Still, my rage simmered and when G— caught up, I turned upon her with a hiss. How could the foolish old woman allow this to happen? How dare *SHE* be allowed in *my* garden? I was told that SHE was to be confined. Why was SHE not confined?

G— bowed her head. Oh! that I could have struck it from her shoulders!

"SHE is not a prisoner, Majesty. SHE takes the air each afternoon, for her health."

Was there a subtle emphasis in her speech? *SHE* is not prisoner . . . as I am, or might be? I have played this over so many times since, I begin to doubt the veracity of my memory. Why, this very evening when G— brought me supper, her face was as calm and equanimous as stone. My repast was meagre: a slice of bread and a sliver of cold smoked pork, with three fresh figs on the side. When I questioned it, G— frowned.

"You said you were of low appetite this evening, Majesty."

Had I said such a thing? I could not remember, but was not about to admit as much. I dismissed her, ate my paltry supper and remained unsatisfied. SHE will be given all the food she wants, I will warrant. SHE will wish for nothing.

I attempted to leave my quarters again tonight. My young, pretty guard stood to attention when I opened the door but took a step to block my path when I made to leave.

"I have orders to see you remain safe, M'lady."

He spoke nervously but the grip on his sabre was firm. I moved forward and again he blocked my way, this time coming close enough for his leg to brush against my skirts. His beardless face flushed. Please, he begged. It was not safe for me to walk the halls on my own. I bade him accompany me if that were the case but he responded that he must stay at his post, that I must — *must!* — stay in my quarters.

I smiled in my most charming fashion. "Then perhaps," I mused, "you might like to accompany me there."

He took a backward step, stammered "M'lady," in such a high-pitched voice I felt like strangling the poor whelp. Instead, I smiled and smiled some more. I was lonely, I told him, offering my hand for him to take. So lonely and in sore need of companionship.

He is very young, my pretty guard, full of speed with stamina yet to make a satisfactory appearance. But he is sweet as well and did all that I bade him with an endearing keenness. If it were not for the current circumstances, I might have groomed him for a lover. As matters stand now, I doubt that I shall see him again.

I feigned sleep until I heard his breathing deepen, then slipped from the bed. I intended to return to the Queen's Chambers or, more correctly, to the small alcove to spy upon HER and — although I scarce cared to admit it to myself — to make sure that SHE was sleeping alone.

I did not get that far.

A guard whom I recognised from my husband's private

retinue, big and burly with a chestnut beard, almost walked into me as he rounded a corner.

"Majesty," he could not quite stop himself from blurting, his eyes wide. Quickly, the man collected himself. "M'lady," he said, more forcefully. "May I escort you back to your quarters? You appear lost."

It was not a question. Nor a choice.

Upon our return, a rat came scuttling down the hall towards us. The bearded seargent attempted to stamp the rodent underfoot but it was too quick for him. I buried a smile in the cuff of my gown.

We caught the young guard exiting my quarters, shirt agape and boots in hand. I noticed a fresh runnel of blood on his foot, as though from a small but ferocious bite. My escort raised an eyebrow at the boy, who muttered a story about checking my rooms for vermin, before sending him on his way. The man apologised for appointing me such insufficient protection. He would himself remain outside my door for the remainder of the night so that I should feel safe within. If there was anything further I required, I need only ask. There was no need for me to wander alone through the palace at night, he told me.

No need to wander at all, his sharp eyes underscored.

It has been more than a week since I have seen my pretty guard. An old soldier, grizzled and taciturn, has taken his place. My hope is that the lad has merely been banished, but I fear for his tongue, not to mention his other parts, as I have no doubt that my husband was informed of our transgression. The King commands absolute devotion from his personal guard; they hold all of his secrets, and keep none from him. I can trust not a man of them.

Neither do I trust G— with her flat eyes and mouth now set in a perpetual line. I am sure she must report to my husband and his advisors. I have not been permitted to leave my quarters since that afternoon in the garden. It is for my own protection, G— assures me — and, of course, for the protection of the Crown. If it were to become common knowledge, this plot to produce a legitimate heir, then we would all of us pay dearly. Without an heir, my husband's younger brother would petition to install his eldest son on the throne, a squirrelly weasel-faced boy and my husband's least favourite nephew, with himself as regent.

I know she speaks the truth. This does not ease the rub of it.

How much simpler things would be if a Queen would be permitted to rule in her own right. There would be no need for such subterfuge with two capable daughters waiting in the wings. Ah, but there we find the concern: *capable*. A woman could never rule with the same strength, the same cool measure and iron will that a man commands. Better for us to stand beside the throne, to whisper our influence in kingly ears who, if they are wise, will take our counsel into consideration. Certainly, I would not wish to be King, with the responsibility and wisdom that entails; I cannot imagine any woman who would. Leave it to the men. Let them rule the world as we manage our household affairs. We each leave footprints as befit the natural size and shape of our feet.

But I digress with such useless musings.

Let me instead record here that of which I am now resolved: if I am to be refused the freedom of walking out of doors, then no other shall be permitted the liberty of frequenting these quarters while I am in residence. G— has already been instructed to leave my meals in the ante-room. I will make my own fire and dress myself without her aid. Not that I have reason to dress, if all there is to do is stare out of the window, unpick my embroidery, and read my books until I am sick to death of the taste of their words in my mouth.

There is, however, a strange liberty to this existence. I am alone, unwatched and unremarked upon, with no appointments to keep nor petitioners to entertain. I feel almost like a child again, as I was before my mother died. My days belong to me alone; how grating that I am unable to do precisely what I want with them.

I have the rats for company at least. The large one with the silver streak down his back has mustered up a battalion of cohorts and they continue to bring me offerings from their travels. Tonight they brought me an ivory comb entwined with a single golden hair. I can guess to whom it belongs but not why the rats laid it at my feet. What is ~~my mother~~ the hazel tree trying to tell me? I burnt the hair in the fire, enjoying the acrid smell of its too-brief immolation.

One rodent, a small grey creature with aristocratic paws, is in the habit of fetching me little cakes. Such treats have never accompanied any of the meals that I have received from G— and I devour them with relish, content in the knowledge that one less delicacy will pass HER lips. Perhaps the rat has even crawled over the remainder of the cakes, gnawing at the edges and leaving pawprints in the frosting. I relish the notion that all the rest have been thrown away and I am the only one to taste them!

If only my new friends would refrain from nipping my feet to announce their nocturnal visitations. My toes are covered with wounds, some of which are healing less well than others. I asked G— to bring me a pair of fur slippers and she returned with a pair made from softest ermine. It is a relief to slide my poor, bleeding feet into them each day. I do not admonish the rats too harshly; they are my allies and cannot, after all, help their nature.

Last night I dreamed that my step-sister paid me another visit in her cloak and veil, which she did not remove as we strolled in the gardens. I thought at first that they were ~~the Queen's gardens~~ my gardens but, as we walked, I saw flowers that I did not recognise and heard strange bird-song among the trees. Before long, we were meandering through a hedge-maze, the walls of which soared higher than our heads. I do not remember much of what was said between us but I woke with an odd feeling of trepidation and longing.

Of course, I wonder now if there was not some magic to it, as M— indeed came to see me again this afternoon. She was veiled as before, and as in my dream, but her cloak this time was a drab brown. She reminded me of a house sparrow, flitting about from window to chair, refusing to sit still and take tea.

"Look at this place!" she burst out at one point, before admonishing me to allow G— to come in and clean from time to time. I reminded her that I have not forgotten how to clean for myself, and that I shall see to it when I feel the need. She wrinkled her nose at my clothes left in limp piles all over the floor, and at the dishes, which I had not yet returned to the ante-room for collection. I like to leave a portion for the rats to eat, by way of gratitude for their service.

When I asked her why she had come, the look she dared bestow upon me was so steeped in pity that I wanted to claw her eyes from her skull. G— was concerned for my health, M— said, making no attempt to hide her survey of my quarters. She pointed to the hazel twig that I keep propped up in an empty wine jug. Its leaves are still green, if wilted. But they have not fallen.

"What is that wretched thing?" she asked.

"My garden," I told her. "What garden I am allowed to have."

M— shook her head in disapproval. She told me that I have a beautiful garden in which I shall walk once again if only I am clever.

I glowered at her. I am not as stupid as she thinks. I have guessed her plans, I said: she will have her straw-haired slattern installed in my place, with the precious baby boy as bride price and M—'s mouth whispering constantly in her ear. But what did she hope to accomplish, I wanted to know. What did she think it would gain her in the long run?

My step-sister blanched. She has told me already, she said, she did not wish the girl to be here *at all*, let alone on the throne. She had wanted my help to remove her but now — and here she threw her arms in the air, gesturing at the disarray that surrounded us — she could see she was mistaken in her petition. What influence might a mad woman possibly possess?

"More than you," I snapped. Her jealousy was obvious, and pathetic. She has always been jealous of me, I reminded her; she has always wanted what was mine. "Careful how you step, sister. Should I desire it, I can take everything that is yours."

M— was furious. What more could I take, she demanded to know. Banished to an impoverished county with a husband who seems determined to throw every last copper he owns onto the card table. Forbidden by royal decree to see her own mother, for her own mother forbidden to attend the court or visit the home of any noble family, including her own. Have I not had revenge enough?

"Go back to your household," I said. "I shall send your bitch to heel once she has whelped."

At that, M— flushed and raised a hand, but I took hold of her wrist before she could strike. My fingers dug into her soft flesh until tears sparked at her eyes.

"You would dare contemplate violence against your Queen?" After one final squeeze, I cast her wrist aside and watched with no small amount of satisfaction as she rubbed at her injury. "I could have you executed for that."

M— straightened and smoothed her skirts. "As I understand it, *M'lady*, you are not Queen. *Not while you live in these rooms.*"

I said nothing more but waited until the wretched woman took her leave and silence again settled in the room. Then I picked up the first item that came to hand — a small pewter goblet — and threw it against the wall. It made a somewhat satisfying clatter but I wanted more. A glass soon followed, then plates and a candlestick and anything else not fastened down. It was all *extremely* satisfying. Shortly afterward, as I sat slumped in a chair, examining a modest cut on my index finger, G— bustled into the room with mouth agape. Had she been spying on me? I told her to leave just as quickly, that I had not summoned her and had no wish for her presence.

G— made no reply, merely took my hand in hers and frowned. Then she retrieved a handkerchief from her apron and tied it around my finger, remarking on what a wonder it was that the whole palace had not been brought running at the ruckus.

Ignoring her, I demanded instead that I see my husband. Today.

The old woman looked quickly about the room. "Perhaps tomorrow, Majesty. The King is very busy with matters of court."

I told her again that I would see him today. She would bring him to me.

G— pursed her lips. I can picture that sour disapproval even now. How the crone galls me! She began to gather broken pieces of crockery in her apron and said she would draw me a bath, once this task was done.

"So you might drown me in it," I muttered.

The woman looked at me with such naked fear in her eyes that I knew I had caught her out. There *is* a plot against me and she must surely be a party to it. Have she and M— and the girl all conspired together? Have they planned, the three of them, to seduce the King and usurp my rightful place by his side? It seems clearer and clearer. If the Queen is mad — or dead — or both — then the King would be permitted to remarry . . .

I refused a bath and forbade her to finish tidying or to bring me anything more until I have seen my husband.

He must be told what is happening.

He must be told of the conspiracy of these women against ~~me~~ us.

"Fetch my husband to me," were the last words I spoke to G— and I will speak no more, to her or to anyone, until I have seen him. I am sitting, by candlelight, writing this down before I forget too much of it. Outside my window the moon is nearly full. My husband has not visited today but I have a plan of my own. I will wait for the rats to come and then whisper into their ears. "Fetch my husband," I will instruct them. "His wife is in grave peril."

I have written a note for them to take. Once he knows how great my need, he will visit.

Unlike G—, the rats are loyal to me. They will tell him the truth.

They are the only living creatures I can trust.

It has been ~~three four~~ three days since G— attempted to clean my rooms. She has left food in the ante-room that only the rats have eaten. They have all lived but still I worry about poison.

My husband has not visited.

~~When I close my eyes, I can see him with her. Their bodies entwined. Her mouth open, his tongue on her throat. Majesty, he whispers, my Queen.~~

"Majesty," G— whispers in my ear. "Please, we must make you presentable if you are to see the King."

I push her away. Of course she wants me to be presentable. She does not wish for him to see what they are doing to me. It would mean her head.

I refuse to bathe. I refuse to let her brush my hair. I refuse to change into the new gown she has fetched. I refuse to surrender my ermine slippers, although they are stiff with blood.

Fetch me my husband.

Fetch me my husband.

He was here today, unless it was a dream. He held my hand but kept his distance on the edge of the bed. I told him of the conspiracy, of my fears of poisoned food, but he merely shook his head. His eyes were sad, and seemed somewhat — fearful? Of his wife? What terror can he have of me? When I moved to embrace him, he stood up, ~~nose wrinkling in distaste~~.

"Hush," he said. "You imagine too much. G— is your faithful servant; she would do nothing to harm you."

I asked him about M—, if he trusted her also, and he appeared puzzled. My step-sister has not visited for many moons, he told me. I was confusing my fearful dreams with the waking world.

Is he right? Did I conjure M— and her cruel visits only to torture myself? I remember her face so clearly. I remember what she said to me.

I wish I could be certain.

This morning, my head felt clearer and I allowed G— to draw me a bath. She boiled water in my fireplace and added lavender and rose petals. I asked her if my husband had visited yesterday.

"You know he did, Majesty."

And my step-sister, I further enquired. Has M— come these past moons as well, to sit with me in my prison? G— glanced towards the door and when she spoke again it was in a whisper.

"You know this too, Majesty, though you be the only one who does. You and me and no other."

"Then you admit to conspiracy?" I retorted. "To placing a cuckoo in my nest?"

G— took a sharp breath. "Not a cuckoo, Majesty, but an innocent robin whose egg will be stolen from her." Her strong fingers worked to untangle my hair. Nothing more was said until she was done. Then, in a low voice, she inquired as to whether I would help them.

I made no reply. I need time to think on this, to figure the exact workings of the plot.

G— asked how I would feel if one of my daughters were taken away from me. If they were given to another to raise and never to know I was their mother. I can not imagine it. Never seeing H— or L— grow, never knowing them at all; even little S —, for all her difficult traits, never to have been her mother but knowing, always, that she was in the world, somewhere, and that I would never again speak to her, to them, my darling daughters — *NO!*

I *will* not imagine it.

Besides, this would not be the case. The girl would know at all times not only where HER son lived but that he was being given the best of all possible upbringings, infinitely better than any maidservant could dream to provide. SHE would see HER son become a Prince, and then a King. How petty a creature SHE must be to deny HER child such a glittering future in order to find solace for HERSELF. No, it is not the same.

If indeed, as I still suspect, SHE had not planned from the very start to beget a child with the vile purpose of holding it to ransom.

Either way, the girl is a pawn. Whether manipulated by M—, with her designs on my position, or by my husband to shore up ~~his own power~~ our power . . . what then does it matter?

The child will be looked after. The child will become King.

No *worthy* mother could want for more.

· · ·

I could not sleep, having been able to think of little else but the girl. My mind turns itself in circles, not knowing where to settle. SHE is a pawn; SHE is cunning. SHE wishes only to keep HER baby; SHE wishes to replace me. M— seeks to help her; M— seeks to have me dethroned. All things seems true. All things could just as easily be false.

This morning, I told G— that I wanted to see HER. I wished to speak to HER, I said, and to look HER in the eye while I did so.

G— was askance. It was impossible, she told me, an impossible thing that I asked. I could not be brought to HER chambers, nor SHE to mine. The risk of someone seeing us together was far too great.

I reminded her of that day in the gardens. I merely wished to speak with the girl directly; I grow weary of hearsay and whispers. I want to hear what SHE wishes from HER own lips. G— pursed her mouth in that familiar, sour way. Finally, after she had finished dressing my hair, she said that she would see what could be arranged.

Last night, I dreamed of walking in the gardens. The hazel tree was lush and heavy with nuts and, upon a branch low to the ground, there perched three white birds. They were not doves, nor any kind of birds I had ever seen. One by one, they sang to me in the voices of my daughters. I cannot now recall, in waking, the words of the songs, but they left me feeling sad and frightened.

I remember reaching out for the birds, wanting to take them into my arms and comfort them, but instead they took flight and circled away from me. Before she flew away, the third bird, the smallest one that I knew to be S—, regarded me with bead-black eyes and spoke words that I have also left behind in the land of dreams. I wish I could remember what she said because it seemed significant. But then, does not everything in dreams seem so?

Wait. I think — no, it is gone.

Gone as my three daughters, flying away into the clear blue sky, leaving me alone on the ground below. In the dream I could somehow see myself from their vantage, growing ever smaller as they soared higher. Smaller and smaller until I could not be seen at all.

G— left me by the hazel tree, which is, unlike the fruitful tree of my dream, as scrawny and sulky as ever. There was no birdsong and, on such an unseasonably warm day, I was glad of the meagre shade. It must have been a good hour, judging by the movement of the shadows, before I heard the whispered voices coming towards me. G—'s hoarse scratching underlying another's softer, higher-pitched tones. I had but a moment to gather my skirts about me and rise, before the pair of them came into sight.

The girl's belly was huge, jutting out like the prow of a galleon, HER dress floating sail-like behind HER. SHE hesitated when SHE saw me, so that G— had cause to nudge HER forward, her wizened lips murmuring words I could not quite hear. The old woman then turned her back on us, keeping a watchful eye on the path down which they had come.

When SHE was within two paces of where I stood, the girl stopped and sketched an awkward, ungainly curtsy. "Your Majesty," SHE said, keeping her gaze averted. "It is an honour and a blessing."

SHE has been schooled in courtly manners, at least!

I made no reply to begin with, merely stood and stared HER up and down, taking in HER yellow hair — so ornately tressed! — HER pale skin — smattered with freckles! — and HER tapered fingers that drummed softly, nervously, over HER swollen midsection.

"You carry the future of the Crown," I told HER at last.

SHE swallowed and allowed that SHE did. HER eyes — green, as I had suspected — still refused to meet mine. I had expected a different attitude, truth be told, a smug contempt perhaps, or at the very least a naive and bubbling excitement. Not this pallid, craven child so frightened that SHE dared not even look upon me. What had my husband ever seen in HER, this whippet-girl so easily cowed? What does M— see in HER?

I reached out, took HER chin between my fingers and lifted it.

"Would you be Queen?" I asked her.

Eyes wide, the girl stammered a refusal. She had no wish to be Queen, she assured me, or a Lady or anything more than what she was. What she was soon to be — and then not.

I reminded her that her son was to be King. Was that not a wonderful happenstance? Was she so selfish as to wish to deny him such a future in order to keep him to her own lowly breast? My words called forth at last the spark I sought: a flash of defiance, or anger, or something close.

"He would not be *my* son, Your Majesty."

I released her, suddenly, and she stumbled back a pace. A great honour has been bestowed upon her, I reminded the girl, and she would be well rewarded for her trouble. Besides, with many more children likely in her future, this first would be soon forgotten. A stubbed toe, healed; a dropped hem, stitched.

Her reply was whispered so low that I could not catch it. Speak up, I told her. She was not a mouse!

"Will you help, Your Majesty? I was told you might help."

"People will tell you many things," I said, "as suits their purpose. You must learn to hear the meaning beneath their words." I stared again at her belly, resisting the urge to touch it, to feel its taut warmth beneath my palm. It surprised me, the sudden rush of longing that rippled through my body. I do want another child, I realised at that moment. Moreover, I want to *bear* another child, flesh of my flesh, blood of my blood. The scraps from another's table will taste of ashes. ~~But ashes are all I will ever have.~~

Irritated, I instructed the girl to take her leave. Let her play at Queen for a while longer, although she should not make herself too comfortable. They are borrowed shoes she is wearing; they will never fit without pinching. I do not believe any longer that she is the conniving vixen I once thought her to be. She seems too dim, too weak and muddled, for such a role.

No, M— is the clever one, and patient. I can see how cold her vengeance has grown.

I watched the girl waddle back to G— and take the arm that was offered. As the two of them departed, G— glanced over her shoulder at me. The afternoon shadows fell across her face so that I could not quite glean her full expression and, for that, she should think herself lucky. I suspect I would not like what I saw. It is bad enough that I was required to await her return, that I needed to be escorted to my quarters like a querulous child. As I leaned back against the hazel tree, there came a rustling above my head and several yellowing leaves fluttered down. Brushing them from my gown, I looked up to see a rat sitting on a spindly branch, its pink toes curled and clinging tight. The creature stared at me and twitched its whiskers.

"Be off with you," I snapped, flapping my hand at it. "You are not needed here."

The furry beast did not move, but simply sat beyond my reach and chittered disapprovingly. The hazel tree is indeed a pathetic thing: stilted and stubborn, and now infested with vermin! I told it that I would have it cut down when I am Queen once more, and at the time I even meant it. Perhaps I still do. I could plant a rose in its place, a robust and sturdy bush with an abundance of red and ~~flagrant~~ fragrant blooms. I shall have these cut and brought to my chambers so as to surround myself with their perfume and their beauty. ~~It is what I deserve.~~ It is what a Queen deserves.

G— has left just now, having had the temerity to question me about HER. She wants to know, now that I have spoken to the wretch, whether I will help her. Help them, M— and the girl both. And help myself to a sentence of treason into the bargain, no doubt! I cannot quite see the full tapestry they weave together, my step-sister and erstwhile matron, but I can feel my way around its edges.

Why does G— care, I wanted to know. Was she not loyal to the throne? Does she not see what a new prince and heir will achieve?

"I am loyal, Majesty," G— retorted, in a tone I did not care for at all. She was loyal to the throne and to our Lord God above us, she continued, and she trusted in one to do what's best for the other. This deception was not right, surely I must see that? Surely it must wound me?

Oh, how she looked at me then, her eyes brimming with pleading and rebuke. How dare she confront me so! Has she forgotten her place? Has she forgotten mine? I reminded her that I knew full well what it was to endure insults and injury and that she should not suppose I could not bear this current situation. That I could not make a small sacrifice for a brighter, more secure future.

"It is not your sacrifice, Majesty."

Those words still stain the air, even now, hours after G— first spoke them. That woman will sorely regret her liberties. ~~When I am Queen again, I shall~~ When my powers are restored, I shall see her banished.

I have laid out all the jewels my rats have brought me, and have polished each one, arranging and re-arranging them in the hope to scry their meaning. They are worth but a sliver of the Royal Treasury, but would represent a small fortune to, for example, an errant maidservant seeking a new and secret life. Surely this is not why the rats were sent! I have always trusted my mother's gifts but, at present, I cannot tell her intentions. Were these gifted to me as security, in case I am overthrown? In case my daughters are banished? ~~When the new prince is born~~

I wish I could see the whole of it. I wish I could know who I could trust. There is only so far in the future that can be seen; the thread of all possibilities disappears so quickly into the dark.

Help the girl go free and, yes, the threat of an interloper is removed. There will be no wedge to drive into my family. But there will also be no heir and down that path lies such uncertainty. My brother-in-law schemes even now, I am sure, hungry to put his son on the throne. If such an upheaval comes to pass, what then becomes of my daughters and myself?

I cannot lose what I have gained, not again, *not ever again*. I recall how G— ~~spoke to me~~ scolded me, as though she felt she had the liberty and the right. M— as well, with her scorn and her pride, rising above her station. "You are not Queen," she said, "not in these rooms."

They conspire; I know they do. They would have me play this role as liberator only to turn it against me, to turn my husband against me. ~~They would~~

I am so confused and the wine G— left with my supper has only addled my brain. I will think clearer on this in the morning.

I must think clearer.

I need to write down the dream from which I have just awoken. From which the *rats* woke me with their nibbling and gnawing. They are lined up at the end of my bed, the covers sloughed off in a tangle on the floor, and my toes are bleeding again. I have not slept long; the bedside candle is still an inch from guttering.

I do not wish to forget my dream.

There was my mother, or at least a woman I took to be my mother, for I have not been able to picture her face for many years. We were in the bedroom of my father's house, standing by her dresser (except it was *my* dresser, the one with the carved marble top; the Queen's dresser) as she pulled jewel after jewel from the drawers and passed them over to me.

This is for wisdom, she said, and this is for power, and this is for love, and this is for solace — and so on, and on — but each time she laid a jewel into my palm it changed form, becoming a dried leaf, or a pebble, or a bloated toad that croaked once and hopped from my hands. I could not hold on to any of the jewels and the woman who was my mother shook her head in reproof.

It is not my fault, I tried to tell her, but the words lodged in my throat and would not leave.

My feet hurt and when I looked down I saw that I was wearing gold slippers, shiny and too small, and they grew even smaller as I watched, welling with thick, dark blood. Again my mother shook her head.

You left me, I fought to say. You left me, and yet you will not leave me be.

The words were still in my mouth when I woke, bitter and cold.

The rats are all looking at me and I see now that they have

ferreted out the pieces of jewellery I had hidden around my quarters. The large, silver-striped rat is sitting on the windowsill, squeaking at me. It holds something glittery in its paws.

I suppose I shall not be permitted to sleep again until I answer its summons.

Oh! It is done. It is over. Now I wait — how much I have waited these past moons; how patient I have been! — for my husband to attend me, as surely he must. I am his Queen and will need to be informed as to how the *situation* has been resolved. He will find me blameless in this, of that I am certain.

The grey light of dawn filters into these quarters and still no word. I tried to speak to the guard again, to at least see if he has returned, but the outer door remains locked. It has never been locked in all the time I have been here. I am a Queen, not a prisoner, as G— often told me.

G—. Where is she now?

~~I have done the right thing. I know that I have done the right thing.~~

I shall write down all that has happened here, while I am waiting. I need to keep my thoughts in a straight line, for I shall be asked about my role in this business.

I shall start ~~at the beginning~~ with the rats. I studiously ignored them while recording my dream, so fresh and vivid my recollection was, so significant it seemed to me upon waking. Although it is faded now and, even reading back upon my words, all import has vanished. All the while, however, they chittered and squeaked until finally I set aside my quill, heaved myself from the bed, and made my way over to the window where the silver-streaked rat waited. In its paws it clutched a large brooch, a cluster of rubies forming a flower at its centre.

It must have been well after midnight but, with the moon nearing her fullest, the courtyard below was illuminated well enough for me to spy three huddled figures scuttling across the cobblestones. They moved slowly — so as to be quiet, I presumed, but also because one of their number was clearly past the point of haste. They were right below me. If they had glanced skywards, they would likely have seen me at the window. Indeed, had I opened the casement, I might have called out to them in tones barely rising above a whisper. I might have taken the trinkets the rats had brought me and thrown them down, a rain of wealth and promise for a mother-to-be.

~~I might have done many things. And even now, as I wait alone with doubt gnawing at my stomach, I wonder if I have chosen ill. If I should have opened the window after all, if I should indeed have blessed the girl with~~

Had I such riches when I was young, what fortune would I have pursued? Would I have absconded from my father's house? Would I have forged my own bold way in the world? ~~But if I have *not* forged my own way in the world already, then what is it I have done?~~

Why did my mother not gift me with such a choice? Why was it only slippers and gowns and the hand of a prince to catch? Did she think such a situation would ensure my safety? Bring me happiness? Was she afraid for me? ~~I am afraid for myself.~~

I watched, motionless and mute, as the three figures reached the far side of the courtyard. Were there horses waiting beyond the walls? A carriage perhaps — for surely SHE could not ride in her condition, not even side-saddle. Who else did they enlist to their cause? My husband, I am sure, shall ferret out all *traitors*. ~~But why is it taking so long for him to send for me? Does he doubt my innocence? Does he believe I played a part in the conspiracy, rather than seeing to thwart it?~~

She stumbled at one point and, if I close my eyes, I can still summon to mind the picture of it. How she fell to one knee — or, no, rather how she *almost* fell, the other women grasping her arms before she touched the ground. How they helped her to her feet. I can see her hands cradling her belly — I imagine that they shook and she pressed them close to still them. Her hood had fallen back. Her yellow hair shone in the moonlight.

The silver-streaked rat nipped hard at my wrist. Enraged, I

struck the creature so hard that it flew from the sill and landed with a small, pained squeak near the fireplace. I do not know where it has taken itself, nor where the other rats may be. ~~But I did see it limp away and was relieved. Relieved! That a rodent did not perish beneath my hand! What a soft, silly woman I have become!~~

I digress.

The grizzled old guard did not appear surprised when I opened the door to my quarters and stepped into the hall. Perhaps he had been anticipating an escape all these nights and felt himself at last rewarded! He moved immediately to block my path, but I shook my head and commanded him to fetch his superior.

"There are thieves in this house," I snapped when he began to make his refusal, "and that which is most precious to the Crown is being stolen away beneath our noses."

The guard stared at me, confused and clearly sceptical. He stated that he could not leave me. That my protection was his sole duty.

I held his gaze, my jaw tightening. I could not allow my wrath to come to the boil. I needed this man to *hear* me.

"Do as I request," I said, "or it will be your head on a pike come dawn. They leave by the West Gate."

Still he hesitated, so I lowered my head and stared instead at his well-polished boots.

"Upon my honour," I assured him, "I shall not leave these rooms while you are gone."

Then I stepped back into my ante-chamber.

After a moment, he closed the door gently behind me and I heard, for the first time, a key turning in the lock. The tumblers fell, as heavy as bones, and then came the echo of the guard's footfalls as he marched swiftly down the hall.

When I returned to my bedchamber, the rats were gone, leaving their trinkets scattered about the floor. I picked them up, one by one, and returned them to the drawers where I kept them, hidden beneath shawls and gloves and petticoats. ~~I might need them one day.~~ They might still be needed one day.

I donned my robe and pinned up my hair as best I could before taking my place at the window once more. I expected the women to be brought back the same way they had fled and wished *this* time to tap upon the glass to draw their attention. I wished for them to see me. *I wished them to know.*

I am Queen. *I shall always be Queen.*

But they have not been brought back, at least not across the little courtyard beneath my quarters, and I grow weary of waiting. Once I am returned to my rightful place, I will destroy this journal. Burn it to ash. It is too dangerous to be left intact. Until then, I shall keep it safe to show my husband. These honest pages *prove* that I am *blameless*. That I took no part in M—'s conspiracy. It will not be long, I am certain. He will send for me soon.

The room is quiet; there is not even the squeak or scuttle of a rat to keep me company. For the first time, the walls feel too close about me.

I shall write no more until I am free.

~~It is late morning and still no one has come to~~
~~No. No.~~
My promise I will keep: I shall write no more *UNTIL I AM FREE*.

www.ingramcontent.com/pod-product-compliance
Lightning Source LLC
Chambersburg PA
CBHW030847200726
48285CB00007B/2580